# HARRY AND THE HAUNTED HOUSE

## BY MARK SCHLICHTING

One day my dog, Spot, and I were playing ball with my friends
Amy, Earl, and Stinky. Earl threw one of his famous curve balls,
and I hit it, <u>smack</u>, over Stinky's head and right through a window
of the old house down the street.

"Oh-Ohhh," said Earl. "<u>Now</u> you've done it Harry.
That house is haunted."

"Who's going to get my ball?" cried Stinky. Earl said, "Harry should get it because he hit it too hard." I said, "Stinky should have caught it." Stinky said, "Earl threw it too hard."

Amy said, "This argument is stupid."

"That house is creepy!" said Earl. "It has ghosts!"

"I heard that a witch used to live there!" said Stinky.

They thought I was afraid to go in, but I knew they were scared too.

Amy said, "If that house is so scary, let's all go get the ball together."

The closer we got to the old house, the bigger and spookier it looked. "D-d-d-do you think anyone still lives there?" asked Stinky, as we neared the front gate. "Let's find out," said Amy.

We knocked three times at the big front door, but nobody answered. The front door was open a little, so... we went in.

I volunteered to take the lead.

Inside, the house was dark and filled with old furniture. "H-e-l-l-o. Anybody here?" called Amy. Nobody answered. "I-I-I saw something move!" whispered Stinky. We heard a fluttering sound. "It's a GHOST!" yelled Earl, and we ran into the next room.

"Hey you guys, it's just an old curtain blowing in the wind," said Amy. "Nothing to be scared of."

We tiptoed slowly down a hallway. We had the feeling someone was watching us. Then something grabbed me and I yelled! It was only Stinky.

It must have been a long time since anyone had lived there. There was dust everywhere.

Then we heard a scritch-scritch-scratch sound right behind us.
"W-W-What's that noise?" gasped Stinky, and we all stood still.

It might be a monster with huge, long arms.

It could be a skeleton, shaking its bones.

It might be a zombie dragging one foot.

"Whatever it is, there it goes again,"
cried Stinky. We turned around . . .
but nothing was there.

"It's just Spot," said Amy coming into the room.
"Harry, your dog has fleas."

We searched in the front room. We searched in the hall. We searched in the kitchen. Where could that ball be?

We turned a corner and saw a hideous monster coming our way! It was fat and ugly with six arms and six legs, and it had long spikes on its head!

"You <u>guys</u>!" said Amy. "It's only your reflection in an old mirror."

"Let's forget the ball," said Stinky. "Yes!" Earl and I agreed. "Let's get out of this place!"

Then we heard something coming slowly down the stairs. Thump, thump, thump! We froze in our steps. Earl screamed. Thump, thump, thump! We turned and we saw it . . .

It was Stinky's ball. My dog had found it. Good dog, Spot, good dog!

We stood outside and laughed. We'd been all through that haunted house, and the scariest thing in it was . . .
ourselves!

"See! The house was just empty – it wasn't haunted. It didn't scare me at all," said Amy. "Good," said Stinky. "Then you can go back for Harry's hat – he lost it somewhere inside."

THE END